# DAYS OF SAND

Hélène Dorion

# DAYS OF SAND

*A Novel Translated by*
*Jonathan Kaplansky*

*Cormorant Books*

Canada Council  Conseil des Arts
for the Arts  du Canada

The publisher gratefully acknowledges the support of the Canada Council for the Arts
and the Ontario Arts Council for its publishing program. We acknowledge the
financial support of the Government of Canada through the Book Publishing
Industry Development Program (BPIDP) for our publishing activities.

The translation of *Jours de sable* was made possible by a grant from
the Canada Council for the Arts.

Printed and bound in Canada

Library and Archives Canada Cataloguing in Publication

Dorion, Hélène, 1958–
[Jours de sable. English]
Days of sand / Hélène Dorion ; translated by Jonathan Kaplansky.

Translation of: Jours de sable.
ISBN 978-1-897151-07-5

1. Dorion, Hélène, 1958–. I. Kaplansky, Jonathan, 1960– II. Title.
III. Title: Jours de sable. English.

PS8557.O748Z5313 2008   C841'.54   C2007-900420-2

Cover design: Angel Guerra/Archetype
Inerior text design: Tannice Goddard/Soul Oasis Networking
Printer: Marquis Book Printing

CORMORANT BOOKS INC.
215 SPADINA AVENUE, STUDIO 230, TORONTO, ON CANADA M5T 2C7
www.cormorantbooks.com

EACH MORNING I WALK DOWN the stairs leading to the dock. I come across birds — blue jays, robins, turtledoves — and many squirrels; from the end of the dock, I sometimes see the muskrat, who lives somewhere behind the stones of the peninsula, swimming. Eyes half shut, mouth closing around the algae that trail on each side of his body, he slices through the still-blue of early morning. His tail acting as both engine and rudder, he surges up toward the dock, then twists around to the left and dives, disappearing a few metres from shore.

Writing these words once is enough. More and more, we lock ourselves away, enter into the useless repetition of self, the useless multiplication of days. Yet we know, each morning, what returns this way, apparently different, trans-figured, would not take much to keep us in the realm of the known. It is about that: days that burn, burning us along with them.

What are we made of? Dust risen up, immediately settling down, creates the fragile impression. "In the interval, the open enclosure, perhaps my only homeland," wrote Philippe Jaccottet. The places of writing are only ever elsewhere. Companions of non-tranquility, words convey the life that passes through us. At the end, only an indistinct line will remain, a passage of shadows and light between here and elsewhere.

The tide comes in, goes out on the sand. Feet sink into it and footsteps are lost there, inside and out, revealing the past that shapes them. I let the hours enter me, followed by the words. Everything that hemmed me in — the shackles, habits, supports that things sometimes become — soon opens: the immense lake, the trees, the street, the light, my body itself; here I am whole; moreover, I am inside, at last, I am here. Writing gives time back its freedom and space its otherness.

*IN 1670, SPINOZA ANONYMOUSLY PUBLISHED his* Tractatus Theologico-Politicus, *a work deemed blasphemous, which had him banished from Amsterdam. Afterwards, he lived in seclusion, devoting most of his time to study. To support himself, he polished microscope and telescope lenses.*

*During the winter of 1750, Johann Sebastian Bach underwent an operation that failed and left him almost blind. After six months he suddenly recovered his sight, but a few hours later was struck down by a fit of apoplexy.*

Slight mist on the lake, leaves barely quivering. Seen from afar, seen from close up, the largest emerges from the smallest. The finger shows the moon, there, at the end of the dark sky. We close our eyes, just a few seconds and only words remain to make life move, to follow the rapid curve of the moon, to act as a gaze, a road leading toward meaning.

Through the glass of words, through the shadow and light that meld them, the world appears.

IT IS EVENING, A COOL autumn evening. I am walking in a shopping centre parking lot. My father moves ahead of me, but rather than trying to catch up to him, I walk slowly and look up to the transparent sky of this night. A long passage suddenly opens — it is as if I am being sucked toward top and toward bottom at the same time, caught up in this vertigo of feeling the world surging right to me, *I* of dust, consciousness that lives, that will die as well, and suddenly the world splits up into a multitude of Russian dolls, fragile *galaxy-planet-earth-father-I-dust*, held to the ground by we don't know what miracle, what ultimate order. But so it is, a tunnel of life ending in death. I am five years old; until then, everything to me had seemed infinite.

That same autumn, one day, alone at home with my father, I see him stretched out on the living room couch, feverish. Grimacing in pain, he asks me to go fetch him a blanket. Then the images blur. How to take care of your father when you're five? I imagine how long it seemed before my mother and sister returned. The doctor came to the house, then the ambulance in turn arrived to carry away my father, barely conscious, suffering — we later discovered — from poisoning that could have taken him away to that beyond of which I could only sense the vague outline.

One day that same autumn, John Kennedy was assassinated. Four o'clock in the afternoon, my sister had just returned from school. On the television screen: a car was moving, smiles glowing on faces, hands raised to greet the crowd. Then the man's head suddenly tilted forward, back — at his side, the woman in white climbed up on the seat, caught something that seemed to have landed on the trunk of the car, now suddenly accelerating, followed by a procession of motorcycles and other cars. Then the scene begins anew: the smiles, the hands, the head, the white silhouette, smiles, hands, head. Then death. The assassination of John F. Kennedy. For months these words revolved in my body. While my family slept, I got up and went out into the hallway, where I sat down on the floor, fear seeming to come from everywhere. For I knew: not only did death await at the close of each life, but we could, before this ending, be killed. Assassinated. The words and the images they carried revolved, without settling, revolved, and fear revolved with them. Suddenly death settled. Took hold. So in the evening, when my mother put me to bed, I could no longer remain there, in the darkness of my childhood room, my childhood window, a window overlooking a world where death, at any moment, could appear.

For a long time I believed that these events had been spread out over many years. But they all took place in the fall of 1963. I was five-and-a-half.

Years later, I was plunged again into the dizzying sensation. This time, it came from a book. I asked myself afterwards if deep down the professor suspected the true power of the words. The title of the course, "Existentialism," had already led us to read Sartre, Husserl, Heidegger. Then it was Camus. *The Myth of Sisyphus*. Sisyphus, condemned to roll his rock up a mountain, an effort incessantly repeated, fails, and watches it hurtle back down the hill. At that moment all of Sisyphus' tragedy plays out, in the precise interval when he is possessed by the unshakable hope of finally succeeding. Hope, then fervour, and emptiness. He must begin anew, again lifting the rock, again climbing the hill. Down and back up, joy and pain, hope and sorrow. Life, each time different and the same, begun anew a thousand times through thousands of little things that are repeated.

"At that subtle moment when man glances backward over his life, Sisyphus, returning to his rock, contemplates that series of unrelated actions which becomes his fate, created by him, combined under his memory's eye and soon sealed by his death. Thus, convinced of the wholly human origin of all that is human, a blind man eager to see who knows that the night has no end, he is still on the go. The rock is still rolling."

No more answers, in me, no consolation, no reason. My gaze was changed, forever transformed. Since life was nothing, it must be all. I turned over the lens. Seen from afar, seen from close up, the largest emerged from the smallest. Then I saw that sometimes life has to be taken apart so it can be put back together, recreating what is here with other places.

"Each atom of that stone, each mineral flake of that night-filled mountain, in itself forms a world. The struggle itself toward the heights is enough to fill a man's heart. One must imagine Sisyphus happy."

The smallest was found again, and life put back together. Everything I looked at suddenly appeared more clearly.

Then it was the words. What I had sought as a child finally came to pass. The words appeared. Not simply those we trail around from one moment to the next in the middle of our life, but real words, the ones we sense behind things, behind what we name. I held in my hands a book, not many pages in it, and not many words on each page. The words took form, I clearly perceived their shape, felt their texture; at last I touched the very matter from which they were made. Just as in a landscape, I could see colours, multiple shapes meeting up; I could now manage to perceive the words as matter from which meaning emerged. That day, I experienced this encounter with poetry as a kind of shock. What I had so awaited as a child had come to pass. I finally saw not only the window but the infinite it overlooked.

> For a long time I believed  for a long time I wanted
>     for a long time
> for a long time  not to die  no longer to love  no longer
> and yet I knew  moreover from a sure source that
> to live  to die  is the same movement and nothing
> else  nothing else  now every day
> in the street I come and go roundabout  I keep
> ...
> Now between the future and the past is revealed
> an inhabitable present, a genuine truth. Freedom
> to be in the world, to live without quality, as
> the very first molecule seeking another
> identical to it.
>
> It was at the beginning of our age, the planet
> earth had neither hips, nor sex, nor hair, but
> it knew with inexact science the detours
> of desire. Ever since, from marriage to marriage the body
>     busies itself,
> scatters, then comes back together; we no longer count
> our souls that unlock anguish, the wall of despair,

to more clarity.

What will tomorrow bring?

Through the glass the landscape unfolds. All is there: body and Earth, soul, and life shaking them up. From one molecule to the next, keen desire casts us into the present, passes from shadow to shadow, then smashes them for more light. We then enter pure presence, which places us in harmony with the world — we hear our heart beat, leaves quiver. We no longer hear anything, and the silence that then resonates against the hours leaves us no longer alone but among things touched, inhabited, named one by one.

The words of Jacques Brault flung wide open the windows of poetry for me. As a teenager, I listened emotionally, passionately, to lyrics sung by Ferré, Brel, Piaf. Thousands of times, the records of Jacques Bertin, Georges Moustaki, and Barbara had been played. But this time the words dug into the void itself — form and matter, they took all the space of meaning. Each word seemed shaped by reality itself so that it managed not only to recreate its essence, but also to extend its boundaries. Life itself breathed more fully there, and what was here opened onto other places.

ROME, FEBRUARY 17, 1600, CROUCHING on the ground of his damp dungeon cell, Giordano Bruno completes what will be his last book. Through a hole scarcely a few centimetres wide in the stone wall, he watches day break. A shadow passes behind the pale, then-soon-deep colour of this dawn that he would like to touch with his soul, he tells himself, entering into the quasi imperceptible movement of the light, burying himself in the silence in which the light surrounds everything. His body is heavy from struggle, his head persists in thinking, his arms and legs ache, the short breathing of a man who will soon have to let go, slip away toward new dawns, into this unknown other place called death.

NOISILY, THE DOOR OPENS. TWO men dressed in white appear. A third enters in turn, wearing a long, green gown. A strange metallic instrument hangs round the neck of each one. Little by little the image becomes less blurry.

Now they are five surrounding me. I see white, green, questioning looks, and one of them suddenly places his hand on my arm.

"So, how are we feeling?"

"…"

"Are we slowly waking up?"

"…"

"Your parents are here; they're anxious to see you. We'll take you up to your room. You'll sleep some more. If you're in too much pain, just ask for a tranquilizer."

The ceiling moves above me, the walls slide, I hear muffled noises, voices, moaning. Then the door closes onto a tiny room. Next to me, a man in white. The door opens, a woman in green appears on my left. We go up, we go down, perhaps we are going to heaven. Or elsewhere. Then slow pain, unbearable pain.

"Easy now, on a count of three."

"One … two … three!"

"Are you okay, dear?"

"…"

Once again the image blurs. My body lies above the fire, there is no more pain, no more shouting. I burn. Inside me, everything dissolves, turns to ash, dust, light wind on the sand. I run behind the seagulls, then it storms. I roll in the waves, my body moves away; I watch it leave as I remain motionless on the beach, holding my grandmother's hand.

ALL IS WHITE HERE: THE room, people's clothes, the sheets, the nightgown I'm wearing.

The first time I entered a hospital I was four. I had recurring tonsillitis; each time the doctor prescribed antibiotics, each time my throat burned so much I could no longer utter a single sound. I only remained for a few hours at Saint-Sacrement Hospital, a large four-storey rust-coloured building, where everything was white. The hours went by very quickly, scarcely the time it took to fall asleep, for them to take out my tonsils, for me to vomit in my parents' car on the way back home. My throat stopped burning, and from then on I could talk without pain.

Two years later, returning home from school, my mother took me unawares as I was trying to push a small, painful lump back into my groin. Telephone calls, hospital, men in white; diagnosis: hernia. *So young, it's very rare, ma'am*. Then the man in white spoke of an operation, of a stay in the hospital, of precautions until then. *But since it's urgent, we'll operate immediately.*

I shared my white room with a little girl who, like me, had brought her doll. Her brother was in the six-bedded room across from ours. He too could place his leg behind his neck, let his limbs float in space; they called that polio. She always seemed more cheerful than I, perhaps because she could see her brother at any time. At six o'clock each morning, I walked to the phone booth at the end of the white hallway. I dialled the only number I knew; my mother picked up. I asked her, crying, what time she was coming. Seven o'clock in the morning was always too late, always too much solitude.

Illness throws a lot of mud at life, unfolds a corridor of darkness. Time stops, suspended like the days, nights, hanging only by a thread, like the body to the soul. We enter into enormous disorder, outside blurring with the inside, the only points of reference become the degrees of the thermometer, the drops of solution flowing into the veins, the faces appearing suddenly in the dark. And with illness, with this sensation of the world closing in, swallowing body and consciousness, fragile questions arise in the mind, revolving around these sick organs, around the frail life that pushes the heart toward the arms, legs, that it could stop pushing all of a sudden and be the end of the confusion, the end of pain and of my existence.

So we get up, attempt a few steps in the endless white hallway and spend entire hours that way. And the big hand again begins to turn.

But questions keep growing. What is it we call life, world, childhood, and joy? What path can be found leading to them? What wire to stretch above this menacing abyss?

The bed of the little girl with lifeless legs and mine were placed side by side in the white room; two small, sick bodies, but only one would heal. One day they took a snapshot of the little girl with lifeless legs and me. I was sure that five figures would appear in it: my doll and I, she and her doll, and my body, this mass of successive pains — throat, stomach, mouth, knees. Some place always feeling tight, creaking, reminding me of its existence, separating my life from its. For though I felt an intense floating sensation, my body would shatter this impression — similar to sliding on the sand, the sea, the wind whipping up — this fleeting and confused impression of the child going through life, ignorant of matter, ignorant of shadow, given the innocence necessary to construct childhood, enter the play, and the rest, to forget. *Childhood* is not being conscious of the body other than through laughter, caressing, rocking — or perhaps grazing a knee, or feeling nauseous from eating too much chocolate. *Childhood* is too narrow a place to be separated from oneself.

Brutally, pain interrupts the play. We enter the hospital, leaving our soul at the door. An exchange. Healing, they say. From that moment on, we hope only to leave. Once the numerous conditions are satisfied, a man in white signs a paper, then we return to where we left our soul and take it back. But it no longer fits perfectly in the body, it trails behind, or goes too far ahead. We don't know if it overflows or is lost in this healed body, they say, this body whose presence from then on we can never forget. For fear attacks the body at the same time as illness. It also invades thoughts, takes up the entire space. Never again do we find the gentle forgetting, the serene innocence of having a body — at any moment, it reminds us that we never possess it, this body that can suddenly let us down, tear us away from our games, our friends, the simple joy of swimming in the ocean.

The hospital. We cannot innocently become attached to an illusory present that opens parallel passages. The game cannot be the stethoscope or the syringe, the crutches borrowed from a little girl suffering from polio; it cannot be the body on the cold table or the colour of the pills. In the hospital, the present does not exist; we abandon our body so it will heal as quickly as possible. We do not know exactly where we are; we wait for a perfect body to be given back to us, wait for the moment to return to our games. But when it happens, nothing is as before. The fear was not alone. And then we know what we should not have had to learn until much later: the pain of the body, the solitude of the soul, the fragility of life. Without being able to name it, we know, with a knowledge that will no longer leave us.

THE ROOM, THE WINDOW. CLOSED is the world that takes us away from our childhood games, from the joyful innocence of a universe built from the ground, roads, viaducts, airports for the long trips of the lives we invent — ship's captain, pianist, adventuress, writer — imagining our own through them. But I would have needed to know it existed; all the dreams gathered together in the tiny room where we spread out our games, drew faces, finding a specific voice for each one — the immensity of four square metres, and inside, a passage to the invisible, to a limitless world where doors would forever, we believed, remain open.

I close rooms and windows, the places of fear. On the walls, flowers have appeared. I count them, count again, over and over, until I notice that the flowers on the walls have no scent, do not grow, do not even die; I count them until they are no longer bearable, these green and blue flowers printed on paper, hung meticulously on every wall of my room. The flowers become words, moving in this space of opaque silence. I listen to them murmur and resonate continually, travelling back and forth across my room, running across my skin, my aching body, leaving it and gently returning to bury themselves in the pages of the book that gave them life.

When everything stops, there remains in this room only small, enclosed spaces — my body and this page, where words dance. These words carry my body outside itself, out of the unbearable sensation of creaking muscles, of bones rubbing against the skin, of organs colliding against one another. The magic comes from there, from words that become windows on the skin, knocking down the walls of the room; freed, they run outside when no part of me can.

I hear footsteps, voices in the house. But they are so far away, I cannot reach them, and they cannot reach me. I have finished counting flowers; my body is at last without pain, empty, silent.

My grandmother enters, holding a tray. The smell turns my stomach. Ten days since I have eaten. She places the tray on my dresser, comes and sits down on the edge of my bed, begins to speak softly to me. Just words, their course in space, their song, and my grandmother's voice. I make an effort to swallow a mouthful. Then another. As many mouthfuls as flowers, as many lives as silences.

AROUND HERE, ELSEWHERE: A VAST halo we can only penetrate unawares, piercing the visible to arise on the shore
where thousands of fragments are gathered — thousands of
*I*'s that wander among the possibilities, celebrating the
dream, the quest. Soon, the stone falls again.

We look here and find only other places, the gaps through
which words pass, and we, behind, leave one place for
another, no port, no ties, dizzying stars in our pockets, a
wave disappearing in the sand, hundreds of flowers in the
head, and the body wasting away. So we must reconstruct
everything. We sit down on the ground, we hold out a hand
to seize a building block, then another — *house, tree, bridge*
— we find thousands of landscapes, of stories dispersed
among the thousands of *I*'s we had thought lost.

We are elsewhere, we believe we are here. Perhaps we
only ever touch a *nowhere*. A shadow beneath our steps fades
gradually; the earth moves in all directions, and with it, our
life, this path hollowing out before us, inventing small worlds,
worlds of eternities.

A book carries us from one word to another, imagines other places that it transforms into here. But the sentence is completed, and without leaving here we are once again *elsewhere*, linked to the unknown which reveals us, which closes us in on ourselves and right away delivers us.

WE HAVE BEEN DRIVING FOR days now, stopping only to stretch our legs a bit, to eat, to sleep. At dawn we climb back into the car, a brown 1962 Pontiac, my sister and I in back, my parents in front. Hours spent watching the scenery, counting the cars passing us, then only the blue ones, then the white; hours inventing games with licence plates, daydreaming, head leaning against the window, or finger tracing the never-ending roads from Rivière-du-Loup to Rimouski to Sainte-Anne-des-Monts to Cap-Chat to Rivière-au-Renard — hours simply hoping to reach somewhere.

And one day, we are there. Scarcely out of the car, my mother, sister, and I line up, standing very erect, while my father, movie camera in hand, misses none of our climb toward the top of what definitely appears to me to be a mountain. Then, looming before us, is a gigantic granite cross. I tell myself we have made a mistake, real crosses are made of wood, not stone. I ask my father what is written on the plaque. No doubt whatsoever, we are in the right place. This is the history of long journeys at sea, of Indians, fur pelts, and brandy; the story of people from another place discovering what is here.

In the photograph, I am standing next to the Jacques Cartier Cross. I am looking into the distance.

The remainder of the trip was more lighthearted. At Île Bonaventure, like Jacques Cartier, we climbed aboard ship. Birds flew around the island; others formed immense white patches. Finally Rocher-Percé appeared. My father explained to me that what actually made the rock important was its hole. A huge hole that clearly attracted many people. But I wondered what fascinated them so. I was seven years old. Looking into the distance, the choppy sea made me feel its strength. I discovered land, islands, infinite spaces.

Although the sea was neither sky nor cliff, neither plain nor forest, it resembled them all: powerful blasts of air blew across, rattling its muscles, shaking its structure, murmuring in the ear of the world, then suddenly rising up and swallowing it, or else it remained immobile, stretched out against the earth, lulling it, letting itself be lulled the length of the shore — mouth of sand, of seaweed and salt, whose strong smells penetrate us. The sea is in turn both a dark void and luminous clearing of light. She alone frees a path, calls out to the open, to go adrift. Rootless, she compels movement — touching her can only be through penetrating her and soon we know we can simply abandon ourselves there, yield to so much eddying, to so much beauty. We never forget what the sea told us about the cave of the universe.

Disembarking from Jacques Cartier's boat to return to our car, we continued the journey. My parents had taken us to the end of the world, of that I was convinced.

IN THE PHOTOGRAPH, A MAN and a woman are smiling. Appearing impossibly happy. They are walking down the aisle that separates each of them from family and friends. Along that aisle, a history is beginning, a new life for each, from now on together. I look at the man, his eyes shine with all the dreams they carry, his body as upright as it is light; no torment sways him. He will succeed, and has no doubt that in reaching the other shore, prosperity and success await; joy and pride will be his, he is sure. He has been graced with strength as well, as he walks with the woman so desired on his arm.

I look at the man, at the woman on his arm; we cannot hope for more, expect more. A whole life takes shape on this aisle, at first empty and hazy; they are impatient to enter it, scarcely a few minutes and they will be alone outside, and this life will begin. Then the wind will come, then a first shower, then the violent storms, life in disarray, and in their midst, broken dreams.

I look at the beauty they create together, this man and this woman, twenty-five years behind each of them, from now on for better or for worse, from now on their lives will be as one. Separately, they set down their dreams in the room of love. Their huge and tiny expectations, and their deep sorrows, rebukes and disappointments, secrets and betrayals. From the other, each expects what can only come from oneself.

I return the photograph to my bookshelf. I touch their faces, hear their voices. Or I invent everything. Places, scenes, love whispering — all paths lie ahead, as do I, where I will enter, six years later, in the spring of 1958.

What stories does such a photo hold? Its lighting, the shadows roaming all around it, or the moment it captures, regardless of the story already visible through it? On the woman's face, no apparent trace of a love lost in a swirling river, July 1948, across from Île d'Orléans, a sailboat crashing into an oil tanker. A first dream swallowed up, carried away by the wind, high waves, the sudden storm upon the twenty fragile years of a girl who would have to reconstruct her dreams, rebuild love, face her fears, and among them, the fear of losing again.

On the man's face, the storms of childhood and landscapes of tall mountains to climb.

A man and a woman walk down the aisle. Never, it seems to me, have I seen such smiles, never seen such love on their faces. Yet I must have felt it when, all of four years old, I asked for life to calm down, for peace to fill their lives.

Two faces, soon three, will form the core of my childhood memories. Over the years the most intimate faces of my life, the very ones that were close to me, will become faraway, almost foreign. Each face becomes its own world, each its own life, with unsettling shared memories.

We see again the childhood home, the games, the cruelties, and when we return near to the father or mother, we find again the place we had as a child, find again our seat around the family table. They haven't changed, the places that were assigned, and all our lives we remain facing one, to the left of another, who in turn is to the right of another. The world revolves, we busy ourselves with our lives, then we sit down again, most often at the place we had as children.

HISTORY HAS HOLES, FILLED WITH silences, gaps; it is impenetrable. We cannot read our lives, at most we can gather names, dates, places, sometimes even events, but *we don't speak*. The essential is carried by secrecy, *you mustn't live in the past, only the present matters, the past doesn't count, you have to forget the past, turn the page, again and again turn the page, forget, be in the present and turn toward the future*. All that remains are small nothings accumulated in failing memory, no object with which to retrace our steps, except for a few photographs, a few paintings. We just gather pieces of a present already past and leave no trace of ourselves. From past to future, too great a leap, too large a gap between what has smashed and what we must rebuild inside ourselves.

So the past would be only happy. A history in which we never stumble, no object ever broke when it fell, no grandfather ever drank, no child was ever hit, never did an aunt's despair descend into madness, or an uncle's into suicide — we never hear the other story, or just barely, when at times we agree to lift the veil, uttering words, even sentences. We say, *That knight in one of the paintings your grandmother painted*

*is the man she loved. He died at war. He left and she never saw him
again. He was called Shawn, he came from England. She painted
him from memory.* And history immediately closes once more.

During the last ten, fifteen, maybe even twenty years of
her life, my grandmother remained seated. She opened her
tubes of colours, selected her paint brushes, and suddenly
the world appeared. A rider on his white horse, a moon
piercing the thick forest. I would knock on the door, each
time finding her seated in a straight chair in the middle of
her space, reduced to nothing by old age, by the years that,
in turn, had snatched away her legs, eyes, hands. The world
was elsewhere and, no doubt, that was what she watched
patiently from the window of the car taking us to the ocean,
from the window of the house where we all lived, from
the window of her tiny studio, and finally from that of the
hospital room where she spent the last week of her life. Her
gaze always seemed to extend beyond the space, losing itself
among the moving sands of the past, in the uncertain history
the hours invent without our knowing, digging deeply into
our very bodies. There had to be another world so this one
could continue having meaning for ten, fifteen, twenty years.

ON MY MOTHER'S NIGHT TABLE stands a gilt-edged frame with a photograph of Pauline Maurois, my grandmother. She is seventeen in this photo and wears traditional Scottish dress. My family must come from Scotland.

On May 17, 1923, Pauline would marry Édouard Mercier, whose mother, Edith Parsons, spoke only English. She would always remain for her grandchildren the foreigner who married their grandfather and who spoke to them in an incomprehensible language, at the same time handing out quarters.

But what about the dress? For years, I was certain that my mother's family had originated in Scotland. The dress my grandmother wears in the photograph confirmed it without a doubt.

Imagine my surprise when one day I asked my mother directly about this outfit. How could I have thought she was Scottish? *No, no, that day she was simply going to a costume ball!* But why that particular costume, which, rather than looking like a disguise, indeed seemed to be Scottish dress? Why that costume, as Pauline had not yet met Édouard, whose own mother came from Scotland — at least we thought so for years; the confusion would persist: *We're from Scotland*, my grandfather would say, and my mother after him.

Then it was Ireland. *Edith Parsons*, no doubt about it, there was an Irish name. Each year, it was a holiday for us on March 17. The Irish colours were celebrated, over there was where the family had origins. Scotland, Ireland, perhaps there had been two grandfathers after all, the first having left his wife for other women and other pleasures, the second having travelled the seas, initially providing plentifully for his children, then dragging them with him down the path of poverty.

It was neither Scotland nor Ireland, but England. Yet that had to remain secret. At the time when Edith Parsons, living in London, had met Joseph Mercier, my great-grandfather, it was better, they said, to keep quiet about being English; people could claim to be Scottish without shame or fear. Edith thus shut herself in a secret that would be discovered only three generations later.

What was Edith escaping? What was she fleeing by following Joseph to Canada, spending, when she arrived near Quebec City, forty days at Grosse-Île, where they quarantined everyone coming from the Old World, supposedly to prevent the spread of illness? What world had Joseph promised Edith in order for her to follow him to the other side of the ocean, into a world they hoped was better because it was new?

—

*Suddenly life turned upside down.* This sentence runs through millions of lives, as if each one contained an opening in which to recreate its roots, pierce this vast mist the years cast over our lives, veiling little by little the faraway horizon where we were headed, eyes closed, hands open, having reached twenty, as if everything could explode, except our lives, all the other places, but never the *here* that melds our desires.

FOR A LONG TIME I believed I had no history. No child-hood. Scarcely a few memories, scattered and mostly ordinary. That spared me, perhaps, from returning to my childhood.

If it does not meet up with world history, our history is only ever banal to us. Then one day, without that day being a coincidence, we enter one of the hundreds of simple little stories of our life and remember suddenly the other hundred forgotten, lost deep within us, that form a greater, more complex one. We then slowly decipher the signs found along our way and little by little begin to see, as our story is reconstructed for us, the extent to which each fragment carries within it the core of another, and that events imagined can never be anything but lived.

Childhood sometimes has too much pain, too much solitude, or sometimes too much happiness. We have a father, mother, brother or sister, and that is enough to create thousands of bonds. When the threads that tie us to our childhood break, we go into life with this initial baggage, seeking to recreate the picture, or else do everything not to reproduce it. Then one day comes, and we know this day is necessary, we open again our eyes and hands, and the memories abound, both simple and complex, each making the blood of our existence on Earth flow. We sink our feet into the sand, into the footsteps that created us, and time suddenly begins unfolding our story in reverse. We undo the knots of childhood, meet up again with our father, mother, the brother, sister that linked us to childhood or separated us from it, and slowly the horizon brightens.

Do we carry the flaws of other lives, of those generations that preceded us? Does the shadow of Edith's secret reach my footsteps, up to the muddled traces of the name of her land of origin? I do not know much about Edith, Pauline, or even of Paule. These lives remain foreign to me, and even more does that of my mother.

IN THE CITY, CHILDHOOD IS confined to a few places: the family home, the school, the playground. Sometimes the hospital, the church, other houses are added. Little by little, time transforms each space where the child walked, ran, swam, prayed, wrote. The shadow of the years draws in, showing the limits, tightening the boundaries. We retrace our steps and already find ourselves elsewhere, never have we set foot here. We look at the place that remains foreign, even filled with memories. The child we were shows up on the doorstep, beckons us to approach, tells us stories that live inside us.

At the end of the city, the Château stands high on Cap Diamant. There my aunt and I join a man. She says, "He's your grandfather," but I feel more strangeness than affection toward this already old man standing before me. *My little girl*, he thinks, or perhaps, looking at me like that, he only wishes that this bizarre meeting would end. So the castle will never be anything but sand, it will carry the traces of a grandfather who appeared out of nowhere, encountered suddenly along a bend in the vast corridors leading nowhere. The child, like the grandmother, like the mother, will keep this man at a distance from her heart, and his memory will dissolve between her fingers.

The heavy door of the Château closes once more. The shadows have stopped going by, showing where the wind goes, where the light stops. Places do not move in time, only the memory that serves as their foundation disrupts them, invents their greatness and smallness, their weight, smell, and even their resonance against the present.

AT THE BEGINNING OF THE nineteenth century, when the ideal of total knowledge became more and more impossible to achieve, Guido Görres fervently expressed his wish: "As Saturn has satellites, so would I would like to have, for the various sciences, a half dozen additional lives, for Sanscrit, Persian, mathematics, physics, chemistry, poetry, history."

Some seventeenth-century thinkers maintained that intelligence itself creates patterns that allow making a science out of reality.

For Socrates, not knowing that we do not know was the worst ignorance.

SCHOOLBOOKS OPENED UP OTHER PLACES for me. Algebra, history, grammar, botany, geography — the world, without a doubt, was there, and much more so than in my reality. The words sorted themselves out in a perfect architecture called language, which inevitably gave way to meaning. So did numbers and equations, plants and flowers, climates, geological landscapes, historical events — everything formed a coherent universe, the world formed a picture in which each element was linked to another.

The bell rang in the yard, the students lined up, and so we walked, properly aligned in order of height, as far as our classroom. Then, seated at our desks, in silence, we listened to life unfold — this life that, for years later, I would see as *real life*. I was emerging from disorder, from turbulent upheaval, I was reaching infinite places, the joy of knowledge.

My first *real worlds* were thus ancient Greece, Persia, the Roman Empire. When twenty or so years later I went to

Rome, I had the distinct impression of immersing myself again in the books of my childhood, seeing once more the architectural plans of the Baths of Trajan, the Coliseum; as I paced up and down the Forum, the genealogy of Augustus, Tiberius, and Nero reappeared in my memory. At St. Peter's Museum in the Vatican, among the numerous busts on display, I would see again the faces of Horace, Cicero, Metellus. I would also walk along the Appian Way, and lines by Martial and Juvenal, would mingle in my head, passages from Lucretius' *De Rerum Natura*, from Virgil's *Aeneid*.

The first *real foreign language* I learned was Latin. The teacher called it "a dead language," stressing the word *dead*, as if to frighten us, to make sure that we would never be tempted to start speaking Latin. Little by little I entered the universe of language, discovering its internal functioning and the gaps it dug in reality to convey meaning. Each day I deciphered the meaning of a few words at first, then, year after year, the paragraphs lengthened increasingly. Rereading my translations, I was always amazed that meaning could arise from what had started out as an obscure chunk of words, so far removed from any meaning and totally foreign to reality. One by one, I unravelled the threads until meaning appeared, irrefutably clear. Thus the words revealed to me at the same time their opaqueness and their density if I managed to unravel the mystery.

My French books held a very distinctive place. In these pages nothing corresponded to here, neither the rivers nor the forests. We read texts by Joseph de Pesquidoux, Gustave Flaubert, Émile Zola, Alphonse Daudet, Marcel Proust; at the end of *La Petite Anthologie poétique* the names Victor Hugo, Leconte de Lisle, Baudelaire, Rimbaud, Heredia, Verhaeren, Cendrars, Senghor were mentioned; paintings were signed Cézanne, Van Gogh, Renoir, Picasso; in the photographs we saw souks, caravans of camels crossing the desert, images of Hungarian or Breton dances — even football and hockey, which were unrecognizable. I opened my book, *Le Français par les textes*, and immediately was immersed in the unknown; on each page were other places to carry me away — as if life, what we would have called *real life*, was not here.

*To the left, the Champs-Elysées displayed a symmetrical procession of stars from the Arc de Triomphe to the Place de la Concorde ...*

*The long streets of Saint-Germain-des-Prés were interspersed with sad patches of brightness ...*

My head teeming with images, I walk along, looking at the old buildings, breathing in the smells that emanate from narrow streets.

My index finger follows the words one by one, letting each one open windows through which I escape, while the teacher, a nun, whose head is held tight in a cone shaped like a church steeple, continues to explain the function of the subject in the sentence, the place of the verb, enumerating the questions to which the complements reply — I will catch up with that rule much further on, when I return, or, if the journey lasts longer than the lesson, will read it that evening at home, but for the moment I am walking along the streets of Paris, dazzled by the linear horizon striped with bridges set out at various intervals, fascinated by the beauty of the river gliding between the two banks of this city arisen from a very distant past.

*They would go to the Louvre Museum.*

The museum ... I had never yet been to a museum. In my family, leisure time revolves around sports, winter weekends are devoted to skiing in the mountains, in summer, I play tennis, and during the week, at school, I play other sports. Saturday mornings in spring and fall my father takes me with him on his errands; well, just one errand, always the same, to "Au Royaume de la tarte," famous for its pies, on Boulevard Charest. We arrive just at mealtime, which means my favourites, meat pie and sugar pie, as if my father and I had prepared them with our own hands, hands of fear and love. Will I go with him? *I'll be good, Daddy*. I am not rebellious, I would just like to say what I feel, what I think, but I'd better be quiet, I know, agree, or at least accept, not reply, wait quietly for Saturday to reassure me, yes, my father loves me, I no longer doubt it. Doesn't he take me with him on our Saturday errand? Sometimes we stop by his office first, and while waiting for him I look at the magical objects — paper cutter, stapler, typewriter — that sit along-side organized piles of papers on the table where I can see all the waves of black ink that my father has drawn.

*The trip was ending, soon they would be in the airplane taking them back home.*

My finger followed the words. The reality of elsewhere began like that, in books, carried by words we decipher, the way we slowly take apart a story, pulling on the threads from one event to the next like a spider weaving its web, a fragile net of beginnings and endings that scarcely holds the weight of lives. So I pulled on the threads of words leading to things, from the reality I saw, leading to another, invisible, but that I felt with just as much certainty.

On Boulevard Saint-Michel in Paris, we stop before the gates of the Arènes de Lutèce. My father consults the crumpled map which stays with him and begins to search for where the Arènes are located. He raises his eyes, incredulous. "No, there's nothing written. Nothing on the map, we must be mistaken." Now I look at him, incredulous. So only what is written exists. The truth must appear on the map, so it is reality that misleads us.

WE WERE SCARCELY HOME FROM school when we started up school again. Two or three friends and I met up in the basement of the house, and either I took my place in front and became the teacher, or sat at one of the imaginary desks set out in the room and became the student again. We played school in earnest, with passion. So much so that at recess we recreated the day's rituals: everyone lined up according to height, we climbed the stairs to go outdoors for a few minutes. Then the manoeuvre started anew in the opposite direction and school started up again. I told myself that by playing school this way I would certainly learn more and at a quicker pace than by spending merely six hours a day there.

Each of the school rituals was scrupulously observed: light snack, brief rest period — head lying on arms crossed and placed on the desk — prayer before starting the lesson, singing practice to close it, and we even asked the teacher's permission to leave our symbolic classroom and go to the bathroom. We made every effort to replicate as faithfully as possible and with all the seriousness of a ritual the elements of our life at school. Sometimes a student had to play teacher's pet and suffer the nastiness of her friends. So even the inequalities, injustices, the unforgettable wounds were repeated, as if by doing so it were possible to alleviate their effect.

WRITING HAS ITS OWN MEMORY. Most often it takes on paths of forgetfulness in me, encounters trifling events on its way, a few hazy faces. Above all, this memory envelops me like a sensation, as intense as the present, taking me suddenly elsewhere, and another here is revealed.

Where does this desire come from, to open paths of meaning through reality, to bring words toward things, and to let myself be carried away by them? Such a strong desire to read and write that I exasperated my mother by constantly asking her to teach me right away, for I did not want to wait any longer before being able to read; in short, to do like Daddy, read, read, read, and as soon as I knew how to read, my face became words, like his. I was finally doing as he did, always something to read in front of me, at first a small picture book or box of cereal, everything became a pretext to read.

Then I began to leaf through that mysterious pile of grey sheets dropped on the doorstep each morning. As soon as he awoke, my father hurried to go fetch it only to abandon it when it was time to go for work. As soon as he returned home he picked it up again, thus, throughout the evening my father's face transformed itself into words. I knew then he was elsewhere, useless to try to bring him back among us, he was reading the world — what am I saying? — the universe! Not one page went unread — history, culture, politics, business, sports — one by one he pored over each column in the newspaper.

The sound of rustling pages was forever familiar to me; at mealtimes, despite my mother's protestations, morning and evening still the same newspaper, the same sound accompanying his gesture — between his thumb and index finger he would take hold of the corner of the page and suddenly turn it onto the preceding one — that crisp sound that made me start the second I was finally falling asleep. But it also reassured me, that sound, for as long as I could hear it steadily, I was not alone, I knew that my father was comfortably ensconced in the living room, reading the unending daily paper.

Only words have the strength to capture the world. When I saw my father throw himself body and soul into reading *his* newspaper — as my mother would say, stressing the possessive pronoun, no doubt to indicate the intimate relationship my father maintained with his newspaper, and having, after many years, given into my father's eternal loves, skiing in winter, golf in summer, daily newspaper four seasons long

— when I saw my father throw himself body and soul into reading his newspaper, I had the impression that the flood of reality stopped and nothing would happen so long as he had not finished reading what had shifted in the world since his reading of the newspaper from the day before. Moreover, reality existed only when *read*, transposed into the words that penetrated its slightest stirring and which restored to us an otherwise inaccessible truth.

I POSSESS ONLY REMNANTS OF stories, shreds snatched from forgetfulness, from secrecy. The story, each time, begins anew.

My childhood. One scene above all: it is summer, July. My family and I are at a beach on the American east coast, Old Orchard, before that place became the reflection of an entire civilization. I run behind the gulls, fascinated by the strange marks their feet leave on the damp sand and by their ability to suddenly fly away, beating their wings as they run in front of me, then slowly rising into the other blue, which remains inaccessible to me.

It seems to me it all stems from there, from this scene so often repeated, each July of my childhood.

At dawn, we cross the Quebec City bridge, taking road 273 that runs through the Beauce, and continue on until Armstrong, the U.S. border crossing. Then we stop in Skowhegan to eat. We get back on the road, crossing through Maine on 1A, down to Augusta, Portland, and via Saco we arrive at Old Orchard.

On the road, sometimes my father gets lost, so we try and try to find our way. *Was it that side road or another*? He thinks he remembers. "Never ask someone the way who doesn't know how to get lost," I would read years later in a poem by Roland Giguère. "No need to ask our way, it's that road, ahead of us, it didn't even take us any longer, or ten minutes at the most," he would say, some forty minutes later.

For years my grandmother went with us. She hardly spoke, stared steadily at the scenery. Then, at a given moment, she would say, "… the smell of kelp," and we knew we were almost there, that from one minute to the next, the ocean would suddenly appear; it was the moment awaited, the miracle of this long car trip. The ocean would emerge, far off on the horizon. All year long it had kept on with high and low tides, with furious storms. And for a few weeks I would watch, listen, walk near it, imagine tiny worlds and gigantic lives; I would gather dozens of seashells and pebbles of all sorts, shells and legs of crustaceans washed up on the beach, piece together skeletons of fish half-eaten-away by the birds. I would touch in my soul an immensity in constant motion. Simply by breathing at the seashore, all that time, something slowly entered me, indecipherable, that had no words and filled me with joy and restlessness; the waves kept on unfurling one after another, a heart sound, this was eternity, this the passage. At the seashore, I entered into the almost nothing, that is to say, everything.

Feet thrust in the sand, I constructed little worlds, infinite worlds. Time stopped, became a delicate grain between my fingers; I dug, raked, hoed, solidified tunnel walls, added bridges to connect the watering places. Every which way paths proliferated, soon creating a geometry contrary to the perfectly even horizon that greeted me as soon as I raised my head. I dug the way we dig inside ourselves to discover what keeps us in our own lives; the world was opening up, the paths unfolding one by one, and the sand slowly beginning to slide between my fingers. Bridges, roads and rivers, gulfs, secret caves — I invented this world that would be mine, these roots that one by one I pulled from the mud in the blinding light of these days of sand.

My mother's footsteps, my grandmother's footsteps — from the lake to the ocean, by way of the river separating them, how many of these traces does my memory carry? What unites us so strongly, beyond the rough patches, the inevitable breaches that life creates among people. Perhaps it comes from there, from this complicity of sand, waves, and the moment when my sister saved me from drowning.

MY FEET SLOWLY DIG INTO the sand that is met by the waves. All of four years old, I look at them sink in, and each wave adds to the weight immobilizing me. Then the horizon turns upside down. Head in the water, feet in the mud that is kicked up; in my mouth, salt and sand. A whirlpool before my eyes that search for the sky. No sky. Until I feel drawn violently upwards, released from below. The sky at last. I hear my sister, so scared that she cries from panic, from exhaustion. My father almost did not hear her shout while she was trying to haul me out of the water by pulling on my too-heavy sweater. Later I was told: *You could have drowned.*

Another time, the sky again, head between two wheels, one June 24, Saint-Jean-Baptiste Day. It looked like a celebration: from the end of the street, my father runs toward me, my mother follows him, probably singing, mouth wide open, but I hear nothing. My father draws me toward him; I see the starry sky; gently he takes me in his arms, sets me on the sidewalk. They will tell me: *He could have killed you, that drunk.*

Another time, another sky. A car moves up to the light, then accelerates suddenly to turn left, crossing the inter-section. His car rear-ends mine. Near my eye, blood flows, mixed with splinters of glass. People tear off the car's soft top and release me, placing me horizontally on the stretcher. Stars in the sky, then sirens.

*Stand by, five minutes!*
People's movements are accelerating. Behind the curtain they come and go more and more quickly, and while each of them moves about in the wings, someone wipes the light sweat from my forehead, touches up my makeup. I take my place on stage.
*Curtain!*
And slowly the curtain rises before me. The sound of engines. An impact. People around me. Shrill sirens.
*No, that's no good! Start over! We don't feel the emotion, we need something to make the accident less ordinary, that incites the audience to react, even to get angry!*
(Long silence.)
*A hit and run?*
*No, that's almost as much of a cliché as drunk driving!*
(Another silence.)
*I've got it! I know! The driver doesn't get out of his car, or else gets out, but doesn't go see the person he has just hit. He doesn't know if they're seriously injured or not, doesn't even know if it's a man or a woman. There are people around the stretcher; he doesn't*

*even move forward. He answers police officers' questions, but is in a hurry, says he has to go to the theatre, is a director and his show is starting in less than an hour, he can't be late!*

The pain in the jaw is so intense that I can't open my mouth. The director stands up. Without looking back, he leaves the room.

At the hospital my parents join me. I'm losing blood, hair. They tell me: *He almost killed you, that director.*

THE EARTH IS INHABITED BY as many words as it is stories. Christopher Columbus' journeys, Ulysses, Helen of Troy, the Gulag, the Shoah, Gregory XIII's calendar, the invention of electricity, Andromeda, the Perseids, bird migrations, the ice age, Michelangelo's sculptures, Byzantine architecture, the fall of the Roman Empire — about almost everything, it seemed to me, my father always knew something. And for me it all formed but one great story, that of Heaven and Earth.

He was driven by immense curiosity. When we were riding in the car he would always point, showing me this, explaining that to me — everything became a pretext for teaching me something. And I could ask him all my *whys* and the dozens of questions that arose from them; tirelessly he would reply to each one, sometimes thinking aloud, delving into his knowledge to shed light upon a few fragments of the unknown.

My father had acquired knowledge here and there, from the few works to which he had access, the magazines he read, the newspapers he devoured, and, starting in 1954, from television, which he would settle down in front of every day for a while, aware that a significant amount of knowledge had thus become accessible to him. His studies in architecture had been interrupted after one year of university, no books at home — too expensive. Through television my father sought to fill a void. This window that had opened almost by magic suddenly allowed him to breathe in an unhoped-for air of salvation, offering a way of appeasing the thirst for knowledge burning inside him.

Every Friday, at the start of the evening, he turned on the TV to watch a program called *La vie qui bat*. Soon I joined him in this weekly ritual. Tigers, elephants, schools of fish, colonies of birds — each time we entered as if by magic into nature, this immense and secret world, of which only a tiny but irreplaceable particle was revealed to us. I saw the unfailing respect which my father reserved for nature, for the mystery never unravelled, since we had to tune into the program again next week, and again the week following. That world, most certainly, opened onto infinity. So I thought that God inhabited it. I never asked my father the question, for fear of breaking the enchantment. I listened to him add to the deep-voiced host's commentary, clarifying a specific point, contradicting him at times, always marvelling at seeing a piece of the curtain rise before us, thus unveiling realms heretofore unknown.

But life beat most of all in reality; what we saw on television only returned its echo. To reach the heart of the world, my father disappeared: a few days hunting, a few days fishing, and the stories he brought back, more numerous and far more important than the catch itself, immersed me with him in the secret. I saw the deer slipping in among the trees, the partridge panicking in the branches, the bear lumbering toward the cottage to forage through leftovers.

The heart of the world — I could also hear it from the mountaintops when we went skiing. At the age of three I found myself being bundled up by my mother in multiple layers before she handed me over to the care of my father, who set me between his skis so that each of his movements could flow directly from his body to mine. Up, down, back up again. And each time I'd see the river carrying its ice, the indifferent clouds hanging over it, recreating above it another river — so much space within reach, the vast landscape of heaven and earth, its imperturbable silence, and I, such a tiny presence in the immensity, I stood in this precarious balance of the greatest and the smallest. Unbeknownst to me, the mystery was penetrating me, breathtaking.

In spring, the snow was transformed, irrigating the earth. Then in autumn, high winds snatched the leaves from trees so that once on the ground they could nourish the earth. Each process was generating another. Gradually the chain appeared, the world was becoming clear. At the very least my father seemed to possess a few of the visible threads.

I DEVOURED EVERYTHING I COULD get my hands on. First it was my father's rare books, books on architecture and art history, which I leafed through, unknown to him; I remember one of them, *An Illustrated Handbook of Art History*, Frank J. Roos Jr., New York 1937, I would read years later on the hardcover, its age betrayed by worn covers. Each page featured close to ten black and white photographs: temples, castles, cathedrals, furniture and armchairs, sculptures, portraits, and landscapes.

Without knowing how to read, I scanned the few lines that appeared below the photos and imagined stories — all those naked bodies of men, of women — what could be read beneath each one? I looked at those perfectly formed bodies, never before had I seen a naked body, a grown-up secret was no doubt contained among these letters I didn't yet know how to unravel, these words whose mysterious line revealed things.

Fervently and patiently I began to practise reading, and my practising, while still in vain, increased my fascination for the pattern formed by the letters on the page, this swirling of meaning that came and went, swelling and retreating. There perhaps, in my parents' bedroom, which I entered in their absence, opening the closet door and sitting at the foot of their bed to pursue my discovery of my father's books, came to me the idea that I too could draw these orderly signs, lines of meaning — as many paths in life as lines on the page — little waves that would explain things, little waves from which one day would emerge words, real words. Meaning. Almost the thing itself. Making existence arise, seeing reality suddenly appear on the page, this did exist then.

Then what I had long been awaiting happened: I knew how to read. Even though I don't remember exactly the moment when a first word finally sprang up before my eyes, I discovered that suddenly letters and syllables were soldered to one another, and from this alliance arose meaning. Twenty-six letters and everything could be named, felt, lived. From the beauty of order was born meaning.

That day, I came home from school firmly resolved to put my reading ability to the test. Reality was splintered on all sides, words emerged, and I tried to let none of it escape: street names, posters, advertising brochures, directions. I wanted to read this world: finally, it opened up to me.

The only books we had at home were a dozen or so volumes entitled the *Medical Encyclopedia*. As soon as I knew how to read I began devouring every page. At ten I knew more illnesses than I did people! One day, while accompanying my mother to the grocer's, I saw an advertisement announcing that it was possible to receive a weekly installment of an encyclopedia on animals. My mother agreed to my request, especially since, by breaking up the cost of the purchase, we would, after a few months, be able to own the entire series. After that my parents tried as much as they could to feed my desire to read.

The books my sister read inevitably ended up in my hands. So to make these hand-me-down stories my own, I reinvented them in my mind, mixing up characters, events. With one same story, I created other threads, and did so each time I reread them.

The story of "The Seven O'Clock Bogey-Man" was among those constantly modified by a new ending. Therefore, it could only be true. Soon "The Seven O'Clock Bogey-Man" would suddenly appear at the end of the street and punish children who weren't in bed at the fateful hour; the next day, dis-obedient children would have to forego all pleasures.

One day, the first library in my neighbourhood opened. So many books and shelves, as many stories as there were books. Beyond the tumult, a world of words and silence. A world in which I could take refuge.

OUR LIVES DEPEND PERHAPS UPON what wanders about in our heads as children, and which we only re-encounter in pieces, in images that are only ever fragments, half-true stories driven by words. We reshape the thread linking the worlds, delving into the imaginary and reality, without regard for one, without concern for the other.

One day the window opens on its own. We are ready to let in the scenery. The wind blows, bringing with it faces, scenes, minor events, others more troubling. The present carries enough weight in the balance of time to modify constantly the vision we have of the past. We turn the glass around. We listen to what has been echoing forever in our voices. We are ready to reconstruct our memory.

Each day displaces the ones preceding. The story begins, the story ends, but in-between the two intervenes the irreversible movement of time and the freedom it gives the memory to retrace its steps, suddenly turning everything inside-out, and this inside-out becomes a new place. In this tiny instant, when I look through the glass of my life, my past is constructed. And each time new moments are added, other perspectives suddenly appear.

I invent father and mother, lives reconstructed out of the fragments crammed in my memory, intertwining now, fitting into each other and so remaining as I write. The image the words form on the page becomes real, blowing on memories to make them happen.

AMID THE TUMULT OF GRIEF, my mother's voice. I am entering the church, hear her moan, racked with tears in my father's arms. I have never seen her possessed by so much suffering. She struggles violently, her swaying body leans and straightens abruptly; she raises her head toward the sky, her mouth opens wide. Through her moaning, we hear: "Mother! Mother!"

A few steps away her mother's body rests in a wooden coffin. My sister and I attempt to soothe the inconsolable. We walk down the church aisle, both distraught by our grandmother's death, by our mother's violent grief.

Then nothing more. Abundant tears. And silence. No other image beyond the church doorstep, where I will see my orphaned mother, from now on abandoned by her mother, the one who never was supposed to leave her, who was supposed to be by her side always. To be there, that was enough. Had she not remained at home, immobile of course, saying, "Do this, do that?" Her presence alone enough to qualify her, *a good mother*, yes, the one we know will be there, always.

Childhood forms a halo around adult lives — mother and daughter linked by the shadow of the father — in this way Pauline was the invisible thread connecting Paule to life. And suddenly, the thread had snapped.

I HEAR MY MOTHER'S VOICE resonating; sounds, words, meaning. And from them, I try to know this woman, my mother, who one day will cease just being my mother and for me will enter into her history as a woman, my father's wife, the friend of her friend, the lover of other men perhaps. One day her life will unfold before me — brother, sister, nephew — in turn each will lift the veil a little, and before my eyes will finally appear this woman that until then I will have confined to her role of mother, a being without too many troubling faults, embarrassing desires, serious wounds. She will remain the one who loves and protects, loves and understands, loves and consoles, but gradually other lives will be added to this incomplete image of my mother, bringing together the scattered fragments of the mirror that until then will have acted as reality for me.

At the church my tears will fill my hands, I will hear my mother's voice still repeating, "When I'm in my grave, you'll cry," and without understanding any better the meaning of her words, I'll cry, yes, looking at she who has been my mother enter through death into the entirety of her life, dying, yes, going away with what belonged to us both, her story but most of all ours, as if the secret of my own life were buried among hers. As if, alive, she could not be freed in my eyes from her image of *mother*. Perhaps the secret lies precisely in this passage from the role of mother to her existence as a woman, in the fragments of her life that I will gather preciously, one by one, after her death — fragments gathered from beyond her and despite her that will finally reveal to me this story, the threads and intrigues she has carried, the heavy shadows, the half-closed doors.

THEY SAY THAT BEETHOVEN, BEFORE *going completely deaf,
asked for the legs of his piano to be cut so he could sense the notes
vibrate on the floor. On his knees, head to the ground, one arm lifted
to reach the keyboard, he would listen, his whole being tensing to
feel the music. Several of his last compositions thus convey a trace
of his desire to make the actual vibrations of the notes felt, this
resonance of sounds in the body of space.*

I take the seashell in my hand, bring it to my ear. Only the
present enters my body. Yet there is an echo, the slow return
of words to my mouth.

SOUNDS RESONATE INTENSELY; BANG AGAINST the wall, against my body. I hear the sound that hatred makes in the words. They burst forth from the mouth, full of hostility and contempt, run across the walls of my room, travel through space, collide with one another.

The words pierce the silence. They are an arrow aimed at the opaqueness into which we are thrust, trying to give a name, the way we give body and life.

Here the shadow of childhood begins. My silence in opposition to the violent torrent of words, words I place in each of the faults in this wall. Only the murmur remains audible; I hear it in my head, a muffled space in which I bury myself, bury myself completely until the other words, the words of others — slings, arrows, jibes — stop wounding, and their racket subsides.

But, while waiting, I force myself to catch in flight a few lost words, to place them deep within me, and promise to return one day to fetch them so they may find their way again. While waiting, I stifle my fears beneath the pillow, sensing that the next day I will have to untangle what the words have tied up this evening, and like every time, I will be asked to choose, "Your father, or your mother, with whom do you want to live?"

Seated at my desk I will take refuge in the *a, e, i, o, u*'s, algebra, the future perfect, the Father, the Son, and the Holy Ghost, isosceles triangles. The window near me looks out over a world in shreds. On the contrary, at my desk, everything fits perfectly together: math, grammar, history, physical sciences; in the world that is here, each thing — equations, sentences, events — fits into another, then another, and so on.

One day in religion class, usually quite boring, the teacher told us a story that for a long time provided a refuge for me.

It was my first true story; at least, I believed it to be. As she began reading, her voice became gentler: "If you please — draw me a sheep!"

The more the story progressed, the more a world opened inside me where I seemed to know each place — desert, planets, asteroids — and each character: *the merchant who sold pills that had been invented to quench thirst*, the lamplighter, the businessman, and the railway switchman. The story of the rose and the tamed fox: *water that is good for the heart, the stars beautiful because of a flower that cannot be seen* ... that we cannot see, or else only with the heart — everything invisible that, at the end of the story, becomes key.

And above all, I shared the aviator's sorrow. I too, had lost a friend.

ONE BY ONE, THE NOTES throw themselves into a void, crashing into space. The Adagio from Beethoven's *Fifth Piano Concerto*, played by Claudio Arrau.

Sitting on my bedroom floor, I hold in my hands the record jacket where I can see the composer's face. As the phrases connect I seem to rediscover music I have long sought; that I had already heard, before even listening to it.

Fingers run over the white and black keys, hands open to reach farther, then suddenly close again. The body plunges into the melody, the head jolts forward and immediately backward.

I open my eyes, my mother's face appears, I see her eyes, a very intense clear blue, her delicate lips, her aquiline nose — her features combine the strength and fragility of the music. The fingers glide over the keys; I hear Schubert, Bach, Chopin. *I took piano lessons for twelve years; my father would come home and ask me to play for him. Then the piano burned in the house fire.* The staffs blacken, the notes rise in smoke, leaving a heavy silence between the fingers.

At school I was taught flute and guitar. I would have preferred piano. Or violin. But we would have had to buy these instruments and they were far too expensive. One of my joys as a pupil came at practise time. On the second floor an entire hallway was devoted to music. Each noon hour I closed myself up in one of the tiny studios. The smothered tones of piano, flute, and violin mingled, sounding like an orchestra simultaneously playing pieces from different eras. I always sought to follow the piano, to feel its distinctive vibrations and the singular emotion it aroused in me. After rapidly performing my own exercises I leaned my head against the wall and listened to the resonating of the piano in a neighbouring studio, of the piano filling this small space with the grandeur and beauty of its music.

A BOOK ABOUT A BOOK only ever superficially sheds light on it. The author gives no key, possesses no answer, no truth more worthy than another. We cannot stop meaning. It is a bird that flies away as soon as we approach, a fish that escapes when we thought it was hooked. Meaning breaks down and is immediately reconstructed. We cannot bring aboard the boat a past still struggling in the swirl of the present.

What have we been seeking since childhood, from one age to another, scarcely changing the setting where the same characters reappear? We wait, but what are we waiting for, if not the final return? We go from hope to disappointment, cross rivers, streams, we scrape ourselves on the stones of our waiting, and on the other shore, are alone again. Nothing has been unravelled. A father, mother, brother or sister, and we look to create the original nucleus, to reconnect with a fragment of eternity in which, for an instant, we believed, arms, heart wide open. We believed.

Never again will I be their little girl, and yet so I will remain. Never again will we live in this place of profound merging. And yet, at the slightest sign, we dive in again, and rise to the surface, disappointed, and the wait begins anew until one day we accept that it will never be fulfilled. So we open again our arms and hearts, with our adult lucidity and our childlike emotions.

NOT TELLING ALL WOULD BE to tell a lie. But telling all lifts
no veil, reveals only the shadow of a shadow that never leaves
us.

Father, mother; how to enter the shared paths of grief,
enter without being carried away by them? How to cross
torrents without also being swallowed, and the wind, and
the certain darkness?

I leave you momentarily on the doorstep, I must turn
on a few lamps, go alone to clear up the disorder left by
the years.

I know nothing of the distress of being a mother or father.
I do not know the anxiety of seeing my child sick, suffering
from hunger, cold, ignorance; the solitude of giving birth
to a being who will only ever escape from us, whom we take
with us deep within our life so that he can go the distance
on his own; this life we create, one day, in a painful joy that
holds the mystery of things scarcely touched, the time it
takes for a being to pass through his mother's body, carrying

in turn to the light a tiny fraction of the unfinished. I do not know the disorder a child creates in his mother's life, in his father's, the dark moments when disappointment triumphs over joy, anger over tenderness, and silence over sharing. Scarcely can I imagine the heartbreak when the door shuts again, and the child leaves on these paths where he can only be alone. So we hope we have provided him with everything: first purées, wool bonnet, fairy tales, nursery rhymes, love, more love.

We hope that the provisions are sheltered from rain, wind, from the mountains to climb. From solitude, which will be everywhere. The child goes away, all we can do is love.

Later, retracing his steps, the child will rediscover the steps of this love, and forgive everything.

WHAT MEMORY IS CARRIED BY images that appear — hazy early childhood, inundation of salt and sand in the mouth, the drama of the tumult, each day, begun again?

We wake up, barely dawn, and the images intermingle, faces intersect, become muddled. We no longer know whom we dreamed about, what this voice is that remains in our ears. In the morning, eyes open, a strange emotion keeps us on the blurry line of past and present.

Autumn winds beat down upon the yellowed leaves, I hear them blow violently, tearing even the fragile branches. Sometimes the walls crumble, nothing left to prevent the waters from rising furiously. The landscape is strewn with debris. I move forward, eyes closed, body bent; everything runs through me, this fury upon the earth and sea — a fire we call passion — and beyond, the path opens onto a silence I finally enter. Nothing else keeps me from filling my hands, my mouth, my entire body, yielding and resisting at once to this silence from where questions appear, at first tiny, then greater and greater — what world order was broken the way speech was snatched away?

Inside every being beats a hard and compact silence, sometimes so intense we cannot see or hear. It is made of each grain of sand that has slipped between the fingers, each speck of dust risen to the sky, and like everything we cannot see or hear, this silence is immense and limitless.

RAIN CHANGES INTO LIGHT SNOW, becoming increasingly heavy. We can no longer see anything but white, the other shore has disappeared. Childhood has closed again. Behind, mountains of darkness and light, violent oceans, remnants of words that float, gaping holes left by faces.

In the square outside the church, the words travel from one mouth to another: *Montreal, tomorrow, departure, for good, moving.* Before me, the silent friend. We have just been confirmed. I confirmed my faith in a God who will be with me forever, the priest said.

In the car, my parents explain to me: *They're moving tomorrow, her father has been transferred to Montreal. What a shame, she was your best friend, you were always together.* How can this be possible? I should have known, why didn't they tell me anything? What about her, why didn't she tell me anything? Or else I didn't hear? Didn't understand the words *leaving, moving, for good.* The next day neither God nor friend is with me.

The friend will have moved, the friend will have changed schools; the heart, for the first time, will have a hole in it, a bridge, brutally torn away before us. Absence, like heavy foliage, will begin to cast shadows over the road connecting to others; the heart will want to protect itself, cover itself in emptiness, no longer to feel the emptiness, to join the shore where we are alone with our shadows, where there are no more words, no more gestures. Simply, beyond the harshness of childhood, the desire to recreate the bridge.

THE WORLD IS FILLED WITH stories; in each life, a number of adventures, immense and tiny. Small oases of meaning created by our footsteps — of air and fire are we made, floating among our stories, after having burned among them. We do not delve into our memory, but into the words that carry it, the images that run alongside it. The thread is never carried by memory, but rather by the sentence, above this abyss — life. We give ourselves up to it; it alone knows the way. It alone knows the beginning, it alone the end. We would almost believe we were led from one end to the other by the words that we invent to describe our adventure.

*Time passes quickly, you'll see. Never give up. We don't always do what we want in life. I'd have wanted to ... I too would have liked ...*

The regrets release their hold. We look at those who created us, continuing on their way beyond the time hoped for in life; we see them struggle with the present, retrace their steps, try to repair the irreparable, recover their beauty, some strength for the final passage — already the other shore can be detected, they approach the bridge; we want to hold them back to relive everything, one more time, even if it had to be the same life, the same sorrows, the same solitude. But it cannot be helped, they will be but one, then will be no longer, the sand runs out and the wave soon will carry everything away; all we can do is love.

IN THE HOUSE, SILENCE, FINALLY silence. Everyone is in bed. I slip under the sheets. I hold her in my hand. As the air becomes rare she diffuses a pale light, a veil descends over the length of her frail body. Are her eyes open or closed? I can scarcely make out her features, but am soothed by them. That is what I expect from her each evening: such soothing, a silent gentleness. Soon my hand warms her up and that accentuates the light that radiates in the dark beneath the sheets where I hide.

She was there, in my hand. I could begin. *My mother is going to die. My father is going to die.* In the middle of my chest, an enormous weight crushed me. Shook my foundations. But I kept on. *My mother is going to die.* I murmured these words, felt them go round in my mouth, listened to them resonate, repeated them, again and again. And I saw the emptiness grow around me, then slowly catch up with me. Then I began to cry.

My mother was going to die, my father was going to die, it was inevitable; I had been told, parents die before their children, I should face up to it, but all my attempts failed,

I could not manage to prepare myself for their deaths. I imagined the moment they told me, imagined the burial, my life as a parentless child; sometimes I even went as far as another house, other parents perhaps — but what of my sister, where would my sister be then? So I stopped the words, the thoughts, and I cried until reality interrupted the scenario, erased the words, covered up the images.

One day I discovered she was no longer in my night-table drawer. I never found her again. I asked neither my mother nor my father if they had come across a small, greenish plastic statuette that glowed in the dark when held beneath the sheets, a Virgin whose indistinct features gave off a peaceful impression when attempts were made to come to terms with death.

LIFE — AN IMMENSE AND COMPLEX matter, similar to the sun around which it revolves — is snuffed out imperceptibly. One day we lower our eyelids, and with them, the curtain of time that belonged to us.

What is a life? How do events leave their mark deep inside us — sometimes heavy, sometimes light, left by the hours, hands thrust into the dust of days, footsteps sunk into the sand? What the child sees through space, and what the grandmother looks at from the window, do we know?

Traces accumulate; soon forming a fine line, a path, a whole life with dreams like small boats crossing from one shore to the other, carrying cargos of hope, and returning to port to find the only face that matters, love. Heaven and Earth united at last in two arms, two eyes, just one body laden with all the worlds.

Then, as luminous as the sun, life becomes this fire that sheds light and burns us with it. Our childhood dreams suddenly reappear in the dense forest, *The Little Prince* gathering the rose that lived among the words. Finally we learn the secret of the invisible.

From the end of the dock I watch the boats leave, others return from unknown ports, holds laden with worlds set adrift, stories without end, images of beauty without origin or destination. "The ships go nowhere," my father tells me. "They just leave and come back," my mother tells me. And they tell me about headwinds, waves that overturn, the river and the sea, slack horizon, the wings of birds that pass overhead. From the height of my few years, I breathe in millennia of salt. Before me, the expanse rises up; this loss of view imposed upon us, as if the Earth were but a mouth of blue offered up to the light.

The sails of boats are the memory of them — winds beat down heavily, or else skate over them, slowly caressing, bringing them toward this other place, their only possible destiny. Time there remains unfinished.

Scattered behind me, the pieces of the story push against one another, push, pull, and rock the very foundations that hold this story together.

EACH DAY, I BEGAN AGAIN. Pencil in hand, sheets of paper found I don't know where in the house, I settled in where no one could see me, and began again. From the top of the page to the bottom, from left to right, from one line to the next, I drew what resembled a series of small waves. Seven waves, then three, a little further on eight, followed by ten or so; in the end I just followed the movement of my hand without counting, but making sure that I had different shapes of varying sizes. Once the page was filled, I looked at the drawing that had taken shape. Nothing. Day after day, nothing. But I persevered, again the next day and the one after. Until one day meaning arose. For I was convinced it would come that way, that *real words* were being born, and meaning with them. I had to reproduce what I saw on the pages written by my father, my mother, my sister — those kinds of small, shapeless drawings aligned on a sheet of paper. This was how, I was sure, we learned to write: by writing. As if the emergence of words depended not on knowing letters, but on the ability to look at the image they formed.

Of course, the first day of school, I still did not know how to read or write. Despite what my mother had told me, I could not manage to believe a person could go to school without already knowing to read and write. But my concern was quickly obliterated by the spectacular entry into the class of a child who could not be torn away from her father; she cried, screamed, did not want to enter; the nun tried to talk to her, calm her down, and, above all, convince the father simply to leave, let go of his daughter's hand and leave. Seated at my desk, I dared not move. Terrified, I thought then that school life was going to be completely natural, just like life after school.

THE TRIP WOULD BE LONG, interminable even. It was still dark when we dove into the car, my parents, sister, grandmother, and I. Vague nausea arose in my stomach, where the orange juice and milk from the sugary sweet cereal of my breakfast were at war. I hated this long car trip, would like to have found myself instantly on the beach, running, running behind the birds, making enormous holes in the sand, filling them with water, then watching the tide swallow them. Old Orchard, a place at the end of the world, each summer brought it back to me.

Sometimes my sister sat in front, when they were afraid she would throw up. Nothing to be done, I was confined to the back seat. So one day I threw up. And I too found myself in front. The '67 Cougar, a model of car ill-suited to family vacations, was packed full, so that instead of forming two perfect parallel lines with the road, it leaned noticeably toward the back, creating a dubious angle. After scientifically studying the loading operation, my father managed each time to pile into the trunk our beach chairs, buoys, clothing for all kinds of weather, hats, suntan lotion, cooler, and the enormous yellow-striped parasol he would thrust deep in the sand, my mother fearing each time it would fly away.

Years later I would thrust it in beneath the cliffs in Martha's Vineyard, and when I returned from a swim, it alone remained, towering proudly on the beach, from the height of its forty years of age and struggle with the wind behind it, while all the others in fashionable colours had succumbed.

The journey lasted almost all day. When my father turned the key to stop the engine, my mother, imagining the dangers we'd just escaped, thanked heaven for protecting us and bringing us to our destination without mishap.

For with her we could not forget that we only pass through this life, in this fragile and — oh how — vulnerable human body. A feeling of extreme precariousness possessed her, along with such heightened sensitivity and intuition that seemed at times to create in her a remarkable struggle. The world split in two: the most simple, everyday reality and the invisible one of friable days and hours. Everywhere danger lurked: a small cold would not remain just that, each minute placed us in peril, living exposed us to the worst, so that at any instant the celebration could be cut short.

And the celebration meant giggling around the table; at mealtimes, my mother conspiring with my sister and me, and evenings spent gaily singing, dancing, horsing around, in short, letting loose!

It also meant that every year we would go to an ice show. Large groups of skaters whirled simultaneously on the immaculate surface, and with them I entered the swirl of colour and movement that relied on balance constantly lost and recovered.

At the beginning of September my parents took us to the circus. My father did not mince words and described to us in detail the natural habits of tigers and elephants, explaining the feats tamers urged them to perform were a matter of exploitation. The exploits of those acrobats, and particularly the trapeze artists, fascinated me a great deal more; their acts filled me with a sensation of dizziness and freedom that seemed to linger on in my body.

I was completely captivated by the risk they took with each jump into the void and impressed by the ability with which they magically recovered their hold. Years later, on the wire stretched above Nietzsche's abyss and in Wim Wenders' *Wings of Desire*, I re-encountered *my trapeze artists* of child-hood and rediscovered that sensation of lost balance that defines balance.

PLACED END TO END, THE episodes of childhood etched in my memory form a strange mosaic, so that I barely recognize who I am in it.

My parents were probably more surprised than anyone that I became a writer. We were far enough removed from the arts to think that they were not for us, not for our family. My father in particular believed my future was sealed, that after years spent in private school, with the nuns of the Congrégation Notre-Dame in Quebec City, I would become a doctor or lawyer, the die was cast. But during my fourth year of high school, I made my father's life difficult; he even had to vouch for my good behaviour, failing which I'd be kicked out of school. At the end of that year my father took no chances and finally gave into my wish to attend public school.

My first artistic experience was watching on admiringly as my sister drew faces, created infinite horizons in water-colour, charcoal, oil paint. Perhaps that was enough for me to experience the sensation of such places and, in turn, the desire to invent them with those words I heard like a vast murmur seeking to pierce the silence where I had taken refuge.

The artist, therefore, was my sister. She had the soul, the sensibility. In her, my father's and my grandmother's talent for drawing came together. She managed to translate onto paper what she saw — *tree, house, vast field of flowers* — and reveal their pure presence. I felt infinite admiration for her ability to reproduce the shapes and colours of reality by adding to them this expansion of life that allows us to perceive a bit of the invisible among the visible. Certainly we were *here*, but cast *elsewhere*. In that *elsewhere* I sought to reach. I was convinced her life would be thus: oils and canvases, watercolours and papers; that she would lead her life in this direction, but life in her took others.

Perhaps it was by watching her paint that inside me a corridor opened, leading to another place, watching her make from the visible a trace of the invisible — *seas, forests, oceans*. Could I enter the words to embrace the presence of things? Could I push back the boundaries of meaning that hem them in and move along the steps of the unsaid?

WE OPEN A PATH IN speech; the words escape, sometimes collapsing on the page, sometimes flying lightly above the world, sometimes seeking to brush against it with the tip of the tongue.

The words come from the sifting of speech; they are its collected core, the silent shadow; they bring meaning to reality — already named, but not enough to reveal the essence, words grow to penetrate things finally, force them to open, and for us to be led toward their mystery, but we do not reach it, we never reach that flawless place, that source where all thirst will finally be slaked, and we pursue the string of words, climbing the hill with this invisible stone of meaning that immediately falls back.

Without ever touching, the words feel their way in the dark, where things are — shed light on this, shed light on that, but they are only ever weak things, vague, already dead, frozen in a meaning that is no more, for they shift in the silence of the world, until we snatch them from it and return them to language.

In childhood, words race without our being able to see them, they build bridges above the too-choppy water, put up scaffolding, construct houses; do we know, from inside to outside, from absence to presence, the passages they invent, the rivers they cross before managing to resonate in the mouth? Do we know the game that reveals them to the child — *sky, tree, bird* — the syllables of a first *why* scarcely contained on the slender lips and the lack they discover at the same time as intense beauty?

Words dig so many cracks in the body from where the meaning of the world flows; we have to close them one by one, start everything over from the beginning — *sky, tree, bird* — for the words to gradually stop falling silent, stop shouting, and do nothing more but gently gather things to give them back to the dream that pulled them from nothingness, return them to the pure presence of their harmony.

We walk in the shadows of our own bodies, meet up with the words that created us, transported by a blind quest that has no meaning but its own. Then we spend years pulling toward us this net filled with what we are, with what we are not, and only then do we discover the face of our history.

We would have to be able to catch the moment when, for the first time, the world breathed a word in our mouth. Seize the precious instant that sees meaning created and all is transformed suddenly, the long silence is broken, words

arise, enter each pore, soon begin going round in space —
*sky, tree, bird*. Things expand, and life along with them.

THE NIGHT FOLLOWING STÉPHANE MALLARMÉ'S *death, thirty-thousand manuscript pages were burned by his wife and daughter.*

*At the end of the nineteenth century, Marcel Théaux, a librarian, wrote each year a manuscript that he burned once completed.*

*Franz Kafka, on the eve of his death, asked his friend Max Brod to burn his manuscripts.*

Memory burns inside us, shedding light for an instant on the room of our life — the first word, the first steps, the tears and the laughter — little by little the fragile flame casts a shadow, so we stretch out our arms, spread our fingers in the dark, grope along the walls; our steps sway suddenly and we forget the very thing that, a moment earlier, dazzled us. Ashes accumulate, but our life shifts, shaking violently, then re-emerges, a tall flame that takes the earth, licks the sky, sure in its desire.

How do we come to want to share what concerns only us? What secret burning sensation illuminates and consumes what it touches, gradually swallowing what reveals it? The blackened pages pile up in me and I will surely deliver them to the fire.

BETWEEN MY LIFE AND ME, nothing. That says it lacked meaning. But it would come, I understood much later, through the window of which, for the moment, I saw only the thick pane speckled with blood.

In the house were only white walls and windows so transparent that every day birds flew into them. I would remain there, looking at a bird that lay, motionless, body broken, scarcely believing in my prayer for him to live. Then I would leave him alone and return later to see if God existed. Sometimes, but too rarely for it to be proof, the bird rested on its legs, fragile but living. I began the same prayer over, leaving again. When I returned, most often the bird was dead. So God did not exist. Nor did meaning.

By seeing the words tossed about — seeing them collide violently with silence and break off and lose meaning — I must have wanted to remain standing and face the absurd, to weaken the muffled walls surrounding me, and to gather the few words that managed to avoid the wall — no doubt I sought to save them one by one, breathe new life into them, thereby reconciling myself with them, with my life that then found meaning.

A gulf opens beneath the words; in my hand, shadow, in my hand, light; the same burning sensation. We do not stop death from entering life, nor war from coming to ruin it. I explain nothing, I do not know what happened. Merely a storm each day, that is all. From the awakening that burst forth, the words pierced the walls, then bodies, then hearts. Each time there only remained small ruins, worlds lying fallow, the desire to be elsewhere.

I buckled my school bag, trying to prevent any speck of dust from slipping in. I got in the car; the radio spluttered voices throughout the ride. Then my father dropped my sister and me off at school, and as soon as the door closed, the Earth stopped shaking me.

AMONG THE FIGURES SCATTERED ON the floor, cars pass one another, barely avoiding the couch, armchairs, coffee table. I watch them whirl, dance, weave without ever crashing into one another.

A shrill sound rings out suddenly, deafening. My mother appears in the living-room doorway, takes me suddenly in her arms. Smoke, thicker and thicker, spreads through the apartment, each room disappears behind a thick black veil. My mother covers my mouth with a damp towel and opens the door leading to the hallway. Everywhere the same suffocating blackness.

The apartment doors go by at top speed, then the fire escape that my mother practically runs down, holding the rail with one hand while the other clutches my small body immobilized against her chest. I hold my breath. Drowning in the thin air, I see everything without feeling anything; the hallway narrows more and more before us, and the space, our life.

Soon we meet up in front of the building, my mother with me wrapped up in her arms; my father will join us soon; my sister will return after school, see the smoke, the blackened flesh of the red brick building, and our faces still frozen in fear. Soon we will return to the apartment of ash and water — carpet, furniture, clothes, everything gone up in smoke, everything burned.

In the chimney, papers in turmoil, eaten away by the flames. Little by little the words disappear, and with them the images that floated are erased, the past goes to meet the past — fire in the throat, water filling the mouth, the white room — all the images rush into the long hallway of incomplete memories, remain unfinished.

EVERYTHING CLOSES AGAIN AND WE remain alone with our questions; with these vague sentences our mother and father set down in our lives, which devoured a part of them, and blossomed in another. Around each memory hovers a halo of forgetfulness, strangeness, incomprehension. The mystery endures.

In the pond of cloudy water, there stir cries, silences, and, in the middle, words interfere, fragile presences that accompany, console at times, and even save when nothing more binds them to life, nothing but emptiness surrounds the *I* that encircles and embraces, breaks each step; we count to ten but still nothing in the mouth, the arms, and the gaze rests on the windowpane. Words appear like footbridges that beckon and show the way.

From wounded child to despairing father, from the child's revolt to the mother's solitude, words open a passageway so that there won't be only silence, won't be only shouting.


We throw shovelfuls of earth over our parents, but the story continues, each one shaking up his life so it will finally be seen, finally be understood; it is still too soon for death.

WHEN I WAS BORN, MAN had not yet landed on the moon. That happened eleven years later, on my sister's birthday. On the television, a man dressed in a strange white spacesuit bounced, we heard, "… on the moon," and magic entered the living room, the universe became more vast, and life seemed to acquire a bit of eternity on the face of my father who, fascinated, remained motionless before the image. The man planted a tiny flag amid a desert of darkness and said, "That is one small step for man, one giant leap for mankind!" And everything expanded: the Earth, the universe, our lives, and that word that seemed to me to contain all reality, mankind. I listened to the words being exchanged between Earth and space, and space and Earth, the words flying away, they too like rockets, whirling around in the invisible suddenly become visible, in the immensity we could feel — did it come from the astronauts, from Houston, from my father, or from a kind of reminiscence from before birth. How to know?

In the same way that I had seen, six years earlier, the brief path unfold from the star to my body, and from my body to death, the road was turning round. More than dust, my conscience was part of this geometry of planets, *I-dust-body-world*, I lived in the infinite, a majestic universe.

As soon as NASA released the 8mm film of this voyage of Apollo 11, my father bought it. Each time we showed the family movies, he concluded the screening with it. In this way, all our stories were thrown into the immense darkness to which I was slowly becoming accustomed, until I felt a kind of familiarity with this world of nothingness, these deserts of cold light and opaque blackness that met up, and my gaze, from one to the other, went from void to void, and soon out into space.

SHE SLOWLY WALKS ALONG THE beach, continues, back turned, will not look back, simply steps forward, skirt and thin, dark-coloured sweater, a large hat protecting her face from the sun, she walks as we walked: "One ... two ... three ... rest," she repeated tirelessly in that narrow hallway of the apartment where we lived; each step counted, while trying to recover her sight, she had to move forward despite the haze in her eyes, walk at any cost, relying on the certainty that the steps would not be in vain; that we would not fall, her flight taking me down with her, but I held her hand, her arm, guided her body so it would avoid minor obstacles; it does not take much to stumble, to lose balance. My grandmother knew full well, she who went through life without seeing anything, or just barely — travel, painting, love of horses, flowers, and birds; a first love died at war, then suddenly four children, prosperity and poverty, a husband repeatedly absent, day after day, evening after evening, night after night, and soon she absented herself from her own life. We think we *want*, we think we *choose* or *decide*, but the world has been shifting for millennia, turning and turning, slowly, from one generation to another, taking us with it, and we fulfill our hopes, we build a destiny that takes on a name, then another, and another still, until doubt weighs more heavily upon us than is needed to continue. Like birds that appear to fly endlessly over the lake before finally setting on it, our lives beat like wings, rise up then fall back brutally, tossed and jolted about, colliding with minor obstacles, so solitude grows and each time a bit of death catches up with us. We look at everything from afar and yet do not see the worst coming, which will leave us riveted to ourselves.

My grandmother stops, looks back toward us. She smiles, with the same grace, no matter what she does. She looks at her mother, dead at age sixty-four in a car accident, her father, Albert Maurois, a Quebec City doctor, who all his life cared for the most underprivileged, this father with whom she would travel to New York and to the seashore, to St. Augustine, on the east coast of the United States, where she would take painting classes; Pauline looks at her elder sister Marguerite, a tireless traveller who would cross Europe, meet Harold Hamilton in England, marry and live with him in Rockcliffe Park, in Ottawa, where they would go to horse races; further back, Alfred, blind at age fifty, Arline, finally, the youngest, smitten with freedom, husbands, and lovers who would lead her to Vancouver. Pauline also sees the trooper killed at the front during the First World War, and that silence that would never leave her, not even with the husband who came and went, whom she rejected and found again, not even with those four children running around the house.

Her body has filled with time, with this sand the presence of which she always sensed before everyone, this sand that carries the traces of footsteps shared with her father. Years later, on the same Atlantic coast, she would tell me about the benefits of salt, kelp, of the time we let slip through our fingers; *Lady of Sand*, whose gaze reaches other places; does she see something else or beyond what is visible? "One ... two ... three ... rest" — sight, far from weakening with the years, on the contrary grows sharp, so much so that in the distance we perceive the generations that preceded us, the ones that will follow, and the world, at last the world that only revolved, settles as if on the waters of the lake, and we begin really to want, really to choose.

In the middle of the square stands a church, a bakery, a tobacco shop, a pharmacy. From there the streets meander, resembling paths emerging from a mountain. Salies-de-Béarn. Salt and sand together in my hand, the timelines dig trenches. Over there, in Pyrénées-Atlantiques, Jacob d'Orion and Jeanne de Caupenne gave birth to Pierre whom we know was baptised in the Protestant church in 1658, crossed the Atlantic around 1678 to settle on Île Percé, then in 1688 at Notre-Dame-de-Québec Cathedral married Jeanne Hédouin, born in 1670 in Quebec City.

Between each date, birds fly and whirl above the waters around Île Bonaventure, which I watch approach from the fishing boat we boarded to go round it, to see up close Rocher-Percé, over there, on the Gaspé coast where my father decided to bring the whole family after my questions about Jacques Cartier's journey, the wooden cross he planted, the island of birds, the arch of the rock.

*One … two … three … rest.* My grandmother turns over the hourglass. Between my fingers the footsteps drop off one by one, the stories that link us. We cast off and the boat moves away. Large white sails crease the untouched blue sky. Wind rises, the journey begins anew.

IN MOST LIVES NOTHING EXTRAORDINARY happens. Simply houses, faces, steps linking them. In the end, we say *my life*; we tell of the bridges, forests, watering places we had to find so the journey would continue. We try to read but the paths are blurry, too far or too near — as soon as we look, another window suddenly appears. So all that is left is to move forward, first figure out a few letters, a word perhaps, hold the thread between the thumb and index finger, pull it toward us, then begin again, over and over until the thicker net on which our stories will depend finally appears. Each of us will invent a face, another, and the same face drawn inside us by the thousands of little stories we live, gulfs that swallow us up, powerful blasts that project us, and of which our bodies carry the signs. A train stops and leaves again without anyone having got off. Thousands of stations, trains, expectations that we examine every which way — we call that *a life*. And sometimes someone is also waiting on the same dock, and the story is no longer the same.

*Telling all* is never but a frame that we draw so that the colours of our lives appear cleaner, but shadows catch up with them, carve out the shape, sometimes designate blue, sometimes red, and we hear them resonate in the green that suddenly edges its way in.

This morning the sky dips into the lake; the shores are reflected there, exactly, both genuine and invented by the still water. We could almost confuse the scenery and the image upon which it is built. The highest becomes the lowest, the nearest disappears into the distance. The birds that fly above swim below, the horizon loses ground. All day long I will walk there, looking sometimes out the window at the landscape, sometimes at its reflection, seeking to enter it. In my hand are a few words to penetrate the secret, to reach full reality. When the light fades slowly, I will stop to see the face of the horizon overturn, the reflection become sharper, vibrating in the silence that also approaches, and will soon leave only thin streaks of light on the black waters of the lake, the black waters of the sky.

ACKNOWLEDGEMENTS AND PERMISSIONS

The poems quoted on pages eight and nine are from Jacques Brault. The first stanza is a translation by Gertrude Sanderson, © 1986 Guernica Editions, used by permission. The second and third stanzas are translations by Jonathan Kaplansky. The quotation on page seven is from *Le Mythe de Sisyphe* by Albert Camus, published by Gallimard © 1942; the translation is by Jonathan Kaplansky.